The Berenstain Bears®
and the
SOCCER TRYOUTS

Stan & Jan Berenstain

Reader's Digest Kids

Westport, Connecticut

After school one day
Brother and Sister Bear were
about to get on the bus. Sister
saw a sign. It said GIRLS'
SOCCER TEAM TRYOUTS
TOMORROW.

"I'm going to try out," said
Sister.

"For what?" asked Brother.
"For the girls' soccer
team," she said.

"You won't make it," said Brother on the bus going home. "Why not?" asked Sister. "I'm fast. I'm tricky. And I'm a good kicker."

"You won't make it because you are too small," he said. "The coach wants bigger, older girls for the soccer team."

They were still talking
about it when they got
home. Sister looked angry.

"You look angry," said Mama Bear.

"I am angry," said Sister. "I am angry because I want to try out for the girls' soccer team and Brother says I'm too small."

"I don't make the rules," said
Brother. "The coach wants only
bigger, older girls for the team."

"Look," said Sister.
"I'm fast. I'm tricky. And
I'm a very good kicker."

Then she gave Brother's
soccer ball a big kick.

"Very good, Sister!"
said Mama. "Very, very
good!"

The next day Sister got in line with the other girls to try out for the soccer team. They were all older and bigger than she was.

When Sister's turn
came, the coach
said, "What are *you*
doing here?"

"I'm here to try out for the girls'
soccer team," said Sister.

"You are much too small," said
the coach. "The soccer team is for
bigger, older girls."

"But I'm fast. I'm tricky. And I'm a good kicker," said Sister. "Here, let me show you." She reached for one of the balls.

"No," said the coach. "You are much too small. You may not try out for the soccer team."

Sister walked away very slowly. She
looked very, very sad. She looked so sad
that the coach felt sorry for her.

"Sister!" called the coach. "Would
you come back here, please?"

Sister ran back.

"Are you going to let me try out?"
she asked.

"No," said the coach. "But there is
a job on the team you can have."
"What is it?" asked Sister.

"It is Team Manager," said the coach. "It is a very big job."

"What does the manager do?" asked Sister.

"The manager manages," said the coach. "She goes on all the trips and does all the things that have to be done. It is a VERY BIG job."

Sister took the job. It
was a very big job. It was
a big job of counting
soccer balls,

of carrying soccer balls,

of counting uniforms,

of carrying uniforms,

of carrying water buckets,

of picking up wet, dirty towels,

of cleaning
the messy
locker room,

of getting sweaty uniforms
dumped on her, game after
game after game.

One day Sister got tired
of being the team manager.

She got tired of wet
towels and sweaty
uniforms and the messy
locker room.

She got tired of nobody
ever saying thank you!

She got angry, too. She got so angry,
she started kicking things. She
kicked a wet towel. She
kicked a sweaty uniform.

She kicked a wastebasket.

When she had kicked everything in the locker room, she went outside.

She kicked a stone. She kicked
it so hard, it bounced off three
trees.

She kicked a water bucket. She
kicked it so hard, the bottom came out.
The coach was watching her.

"Sister," said the coach, "you *are* a good kicker."

"I'm fast and tricky, too," Sister said.

"Here," said the coach. "Let's see you kick this soccer ball into that goal."

The goal was far away. But Sister kicked the ball straight and hard, and it went in.

The coach put Sister on the girls' soccer team.

At the very next game, Sister scored the winning goal—right between the legs of a bigger, older cub!

So if you are small, keep trying and don't give up. And if you are bigger and older, watch out for fast, tricky little cubs.